Sherlock Holmes and The Vanishing Act

Mabel Swift

Copyright © 2024 by Mabel Swift

All rights reserved.

All rights reserved. No part of this publication may be reproduced in any form, electronically or mechanically without permission from the author.

This is a work of fiction and any resemblance to any person living or dead is purely coincidental.

Contents

Chapter 1	1
Chapter 2	7
Chapter 3	15
Chapter 4	19
Chapter 5	26
Chapter 6	30
Chapter 7	36
Chapter 8	41
Chapter 9	48
Chapter 10	52
Chapter 11	57
Chapter 12	62
Chapter 13	67
Chapter 14	72

| Chapter 15 | 76 |
| A note from the author | 78 |

Chapter 1

A knock sounded at the door of 221B Baker Street, echoing through the cluttered sitting room where Sherlock Holmes sat in his armchair, pipe in hand, lost in thought. The door creaked open and Mrs Hudson poked her head in.

"Mr Holmes, there's a young woman here to see you. She says it's urgent."

Holmes straightened up. "Show her in, Mrs Hudson."

The landlady nodded and stepped aside, ushering in a petite woman with chestnut curls and brown eyes. The woman's cheeks were flushed and her eyes red-rimmed, evidence of recent tears. She clutched a lace handkerchief in her hands.

"Thank you, Mrs Hudson," Holmes said, rising to his feet.

Mrs Hudson gave the distraught young woman a sympathetic look before withdrawing, closing the door softly behind her.

Holmes gestured to the settee. "Please, have a seat Miss...?"

"Meyer. Mrs Lily Meyer," the woman said, dabbing at her eyes. "I've come about my husband, Alex. He's gone missing, Mr Holmes. Vanished without a trace."

Dr Watson, who had been sitting quietly in the corner, lowered his newspaper and said gently, "When did this happen, Mrs Meyer?"

The woman replied, "Last night. Alex is a street magician. He performs regularly in an East End courtyard. He always draws a big crowd. People love him." She gave Watson a small smile. "But he didn't come home last night. I haven't slept, waiting for him to return."

Holmes steepled his fingers under his chin. "Has his disappearance got something to do with his performance?"

"Yes, Mr Holmes, it was his final trick that somehow went wrong," Mrs Meyer explained, twisting the handkerchief in her hands. "For that final trick, Alex's assistant would tie him up in chains and ropes, then lock him inside a large trunk. Seconds later, Alex would jump out of the trunk, free from the ropes and chains."

have earned him some enemies among the other street magicians."

Watson asked, "What do you mean, Mrs Meyer?"

"Alex's usual spot in the courtyard is prime territory. It's sheltered from the wind and has good visibility from the surrounding buildings. Some of the other magicians have been known to grumble about him monopolising the best pitch."

Holmes nodded. "I see. And have any of these disgruntled performers made threats against your husband?"

Mrs Meyer shook her head. "Not that I know of. Alex tends to keep such things from me because he doesn't want me to worry. But there have been times, when I've gone to watch Alex's show, when I've heard mutterings from some people in the crowd. Comments about him being too flashy, too eager to please the toffs in the audience."

"And did you ever see who was making these remarks?" Holmes asked.

"No. The courtyard is always packed during Alex's performances, and I'm usually too busy watching him to look around me. Even after all this time, I can't take my eyes off Alex when he's performing. He's mesmerising."

"Only this time, I take it, your husband did not reappear from the trunk?" Holmes asked.

Mrs Meyer shook her head, fresh tears welling in her eyes. "That's right. And when his assistant opened the trunk, Alex wasn't there. He had vanished. He's not been seen since."

Watson made a small noise of sympathy. "How awful for you, Mrs Meyer. To have your husband disappear like that, it must be quite a shock."

"It's not like Alex to simply abandon a performance," Mrs Meyer said. "Something must have happened to him, something dreadful. And he always comes home after his show without fail. We've never spent a night apart since the day we got married. I'm so worried about him. What could have happened?"

"Tell me more about your husband's career as a street magician," Holmes said. "Who does he associate with in the course of his work?"

Mrs Meyer answered, "Alex has become more and more popular over the last year, and he always has a large crowd watching him, most of them from the East End. I have noticed some more well-off people attending, too." She hesitated for a few moments. "I think his popularity may

Holmes said, "It's possible, then, that your husband may have run afoul of a jealous rival, someone seeking to eliminate the competition by nefarious means."

Mrs Meyer gasped at Holmes' words.

Watson said gently, "Have you reported your husband's disappearance to the police?"

Mrs Meyer's eyes filled with fresh tears. "I tried. As soon as I realised Alex was truly missing and not just delayed, I went to the local station house. But the constable on duty just laughed at me. He said that street magicians are a flighty lot, prone to chasing the next big opportunity without a word to anyone. That Alex had likely run off on some new scheme and would turn up again. I told him Alex wasn't like that, but he wouldn't listen."

Watson tutted in disgust.

Holmes said, "Rest assured, Mrs Meyer, we will apply all our powers to the problem of your missing husband. If there is any trace of him to be found in London, Watson and I shall uncover it."

Relief suffused the young woman's face. "Thank you. I knew coming to you was the right choice. Alex always said that if anyone could make sense of the impossible, it would be the great Sherlock Holmes."

Holmes inclined his head and smiled. "Your husband is a wise man. Now, I should like to see the area where your husband performed his show. Can you take us there now?"

"I can, but I must return home soon. A neighbour is looking after my baby for me, but I don't want to impose upon her kindness for too long."

Holmes stood. "Then we should leave immediately."

Chapter 2

With Mrs Meyer leading the way, Holmes and Watson navigated the labyrinthine alleyways of London's East End. The cobblestones were slick with grime and the air hung heavy with the smell of smoke that curled from the chimneys. Ragged urchins darted past, their bare feet slapping against the damp stones, while women in tattered shawls huddled in doorways chatting with each other.

Mrs Meyer hurried on, her skirts hitched up to avoid the worst of the muck. Her face was pale with worry, but there was a determined set to her jaw as she led the two men deeper into the warren of narrow passages and cramped courtyards.

At last, they emerged into a small, sheltered space, hemmed in on all sides by towering buildings. A makeshift stage had been erected at one end, little more than a raised platform of rough-hewn planks.

Holmes moved forward, looking left and right as he took everything in. He crouched down, long fingers skimming over a few items littering the stage.

"What do you make of it, Holmes?" Watson asked, his own gaze taking in the dingy surroundings.

Holmes straightened, dusting off his hands. "Alas, there isn't much to see, other than bits of debris. But see here, there are fresh scuff marks on the platform, as though someone was dragged across it."

Mrs Meyer let out a choked sob, her hand flying to her mouth. "Oh, Alex," she mumbled, her eyes welling with fresh tears. "What's happened to you, my love?"

Watson moved to her side, offering a comforting hand on her shoulder. "We'll find him, Mrs Meyer. Holmes is the best there is. If anyone can unravel this mystery, it's him."

Holmes moved over to Mrs Meyer and asked, "Where is your husband's trunk, the one he vanished from? And where are the rest of his belongings? I assume your husband has certain tools one would associate with being a magician."

Mrs Meyer wiped her eyes. "His assistant, Jack Turner, brought Alex's items home to me this morning, his cards, his props, that sort of thing. But the trunk is too heavy to be taken back and forth to our house, so he left the trunk with Mr Fitzgerald over there who runs a bottle-making business in that workshop. In return for Alex storing his trunk in the workshop, he lets Mr Fitzgerald's children watch his show for free. Sometimes, he gets them on the stage to help him with a trick. The children love that."

Holmes slowly nodded. "How long has Jack Turner worked with your husband?"

"About a year," Mrs Meyer replied. "It was Jack who told me what had happened to Alex. I wasn't at the performance last night as I didn't have anyone to look after my baby. I stayed up all night waiting for Alex to come home, and when Jack turned up this morning and told me what had happened, I immediately went to the police, and then to you, Mr Holmes."

"So, you only have Mr Turner's account of what happened at the show last night?"

Mrs Meyer gave him a curious look. "Yes, but I have no reason to doubt his words. Jack is a trustworthy young man."

Holmes said, "Why didn't Mr Turner call on your home last night to let you know about your husband's disappearance? He must have known you'd be worried."

Mrs Meyer replied, "Jack said he hadn't wanted to disturb me last night and thought I would have been asleep.

He came to my house first thing this morning, though." She glanced towards the workshop. "Perhaps Mr Fitzgerald or his children saw Alex's show yesterday. Shall I ask them? Although, I really should be getting home to my baby soon."

Holmes gave her a kind look. "Why don't you go home now, Mrs Meyer? We can continue our investigation from here. Would you be kind enough to give your address then we can call on you later to let you know what we have discovered. Also, a description of your husband and what he was wearing last night would be most useful."

The young woman gave the details and thanked Holmes and Watson for looking into her husband's disappearance. She took a lingering look at the makeshift stage before hurrying away down the street, her dress billowing out behind her.

Holmes and Watson approached the bottle-maker's workshop, the acrid stench of molten glass and burning coal assaulting their nostrils. Despite the sweltering heat inside the building, a young boy and girl were happily playing a game in the corner.

Mr Fitzgerald, a burly man with a thick, greying beard, looked up from his work, his eyes narrowing suspiciously at the sight of the two well-dressed gentlemen. "What d'you want?" he grunted, wiping his brow with the back of his hand.

"We're here about the magician, Alex Meyer," Holmes said, his voice calm and even. "I understand it's possible your children might have been present for his performance yesterday?"

At the mention of the magician's name, the children's eyes lit up with excitement. They abandoned their play and crowded around Holmes and Watson, their voices rising in a clamour.

"We were there last night! The magician went into the trunk and then disappeared in a puff of smoke!" exclaimed the boy, his face smudged with soot. "Like magic!"

"No, he didn't!" argued his sister, her red hair escaping from its braid. "He was never in the box at all! It was a trick!"

Holmes listened to their conflicting accounts. He crouched down to the children's level, his voice gentle but firm. "Think carefully," he said. "What exactly did you see?"

The children fell silent, their faces scrunched up in thought.

Finally, the boy spoke. "The magician went into the trunk, like he always does. But this time, he didn't come back out. We waited such a long time for him. I peeped into the box when his assistant brought it in here later, and saw ropes and chains, all tangled up."

Holmes nodded, rising to his feet. He turned to Mr Fitzgerald, who had been watching the exchange, and asked, "Did you see anything unusual last night? Any strangers lurking about, or anything out of the ordinary?"

Mr Fitzgerald scratched his beard. "Now that you mention it," he said slowly, "there was that journalist chap. What was his name? Burns, that's it. Samuel Burns."

Holmes said, "I'm aware of who Mr Burns is. Our paths have crossed a few times. What was he doing last night during the performance?"

"Same thing he always does," Fitzgerald said. "Scribbling away in that notebook of his, watching Meyer's every move. He's been coming around for weeks now, writing about the magician's act."

Watson frowned. "But why would a journalist be so interested in a street performer?"

Fitzgerald shrugged. "Beats me. But Burns seemed to think Meyer was something special. Burns was always going on about how clever he was to have found the magician, hidden away in these back alleys. Said his reports in the papers would make Meyer a star and it would all be thanks to him."

Holmes's eyes narrowed. "And how did Burns react when Meyer disappeared?"

Fitzgerald answered, "He was delighted. Couldn't stop grinning from ear to ear. Mumbled something about it making a good story."

Holmes and Watson exchanged a glance.

Holmes asked if they could see the trunk that belonged to Mr Meyer, the one he used in his show.

"Yeah, it's over there," Fitzgerald replied, pointing to the left.

Watson and Holmes examined the trunk finding nothing seemingly untoward on the outside. Once they looked inside, they saw ropes and chains, just as the boy had told them a few minutes ago.

Holmes examined the trunk some more, running his fingers carefully over every part of it. After applying slight pressure to the top part of the back panel, Holmes wasn't surprised to see that it opened outwards, offering a secret exit to whomever was inside. He quietly said to Watson, "This is likely how Mr Meyer left the trunk, but possibly not of his own accord."

Watson said, "Mr Meyer's assistant would know about this secret opening, surely?"

"You'd think so," Holmes replied as he put the lowered panel back in position. "We'll speak to Mr Turner later."

Holmes returned to Fitzgerald, thanked him for his help, and said goodbye.

As they made their way back out into the alleyway, Watson couldn't shake the feeling of unease that had settled in his gut. "What do you make of it, Holmes?" he asked. "Do you think Mr Burns could be involved? I know what that man is like. He'd do anything to get a good story for his paper."

Holmes replied, "Let's head to Fleet Street and find out."

Chapter 3

Holmes and Watson made their way to the bustling heart of Fleet Street, where the city's newspapers churned out their daily editions. They found Samuel Burns hunched over his desk in a cramped, smoke-filled office, his pen scratching furiously across a page as he worked on his latest story.

At the sound of their approach, Burns looked up, his eyes narrowing suspiciously. "Well, well," he said, leaning back in his chair and taking a long drag from his cigarette. "If it isn't the famous Sherlock Holmes and his faithful sidekick. What brings you here?"

"We're here about Alex Meyer," Holmes said, cutting straight to the point. "I understand you've been attending his performances."

Burns' lips curled into a smirk. "So what if I have? It's not against the law. He's a good magician, better than others I've seen. I like stopping by there and watching his shows. It passes the time."

Holmes said, "Mr Burns, I suspect there must be another reason why you're attending his shows; something to do with your work."

Burns laughed. "Nothing gets past you, does it, Mr Holmes? Okay, I'll be honest. Meyer is a rising star. I realised that the first time I saw him. He's got something special. He's going to be famous one day, I can tell. So, I decided I would be the one to document his fame, get his name out to the public. That's why I go to his shows." He stopped talking and Holmes saw the malicious glint in his eyes. Burns continued, "Last night's show was the best ever. A real vanishing trick. I've already got my piece written up for the paper. People are going to love it."

"And do you think he has vanished for real?" Watson asked.

"Who knows?" Burns replied, tapping the ash from his cigarette into a nearby tray. "Perhaps it's a publicity stunt. I wouldn't put it past him. You know what performers are like. They'd do anything for fame and recognition."

Holmes said, "As would certain journalists, don't you think, Mr Burns?"

Burns burst into laughter, causing other reporters in the room to look his way. "Fair point, Mr Holmes. Do you suspect I'm behind this? That I organised for Meyer to be kidnapped from that magic box of his? Just so I could write about it?"

"I have to follow every lead," Holmes replied with a small smile.

"Fair enough," Burns said. "Although, if you're following every lead, I'm assuming you've considered Beatrice Sands as a suspect."

"Beatrice Sands?" Watson repeated. "Who is she?"

Burns smiled smugly. "Ha! I am one step ahead of the great Sherlock Holmes and Dr Watson! I'm almost tempted to write a piece about this. What would your fans think?"

"Beatrice Sands?" Holmes prompted.

Burns stubbed out his cigarette. "Yeah, she's a rival street magician, but nowhere near as talented as Meyer. If anyone wanted to get rid of Meyer, it would be Beatrice. And she would know how to use that trunk to do so."

"And where will we find Miss Sands?" Holmes asked.

Burns grinned. "She'll probably be setting her act up on Meyer's empty stage. He usually does an early afternoon performance around this time. But, of course, he won't be there today and his stage will be empty. Beatrice isn't the kind to let an opportunity like that go to waste. Now, is there anything else? Or do you need me to come up with more suspects for you?"

Holmes said, "Do you have any more suspects, Mr Burns?"

Burns tapped the side of his nose. "I might, but I haven't got all the facts yet. Anyway, Meyer's disappearance is my story, and I'm going to get to the bottom of it. This could be the making of my career. Don't be surprised if I beat you to the punch on this one. A story like this is the stuff of legends, and I intend to be the one to tell it."

With that, the journalist lit another cigarette and returned to his scribbling.

Chapter 4

Holmes and Watson headed back through the twisting alleyways of the East End. The distant sounds of a gathered crowd reached their ears. Rounding the final corner into the now-familiar courtyard that had been Alex Meyer's erstwhile stage, they were greeted by the sight of a sizable throng pressed in around a central figure.

There, in the very spot where Meyer had so recently performed, stood a powerfully built woman in a battered top hat and tailcoat. Her craggy face was split in a wide, gap-toothed grin as she worked the audience with practised ease.

"Step right up, ladies and gents!" she bellowed, her voice cutting through the din like a foghorn. "Witness the death-defying feats of the one, the only, Beatrice Sands!"

With a flourish, she produced a flaming torch from within her coat, eliciting gasps from the onlookers. Tilting her head back, Sands opened her mouth wide and slowly lowered the torch inside. The flames licked at her lips and tongue, but she showed no sign of discomfort. After a long moment, she withdrew the torch and extinguished it with a puff of breath, to raucous applause.

Watson muttered, "How on earth did she manage that?"

Holmes's gaze remained fixed on Sands, his expression inscrutable. "A clever trick," he said. "But one that requires no small amount of skill and practice to pull off without injury."

They watched as Sands continued her performance. She worked the crowd like a master, drawing them in with her booming voice and larger-than-life presence.

Yet beneath the bravado, there was an undercurrent of something else. A fierce, almost manic energy that bordered on desperation. Sands' glance darted constantly to the fringes of the crowd, as if searching for someone or something.

"She seems quite pleased with herself," Watson observed, nodding towards the performer's beaming face.

"Indeed," Holmes agreed, his tone thoughtful. "Almost too pleased, one might say. As if she's revelling in the absence of her greatest rival."

Watson said, "You think she had something to do with Meyer's disappearance?"

"I think," Holmes said slowly, "that Miss Sands is a woman with a great deal to gain from Meyer's absence. And that alone is enough to warrant further investigation."

As if sensing their scrutiny, Sands' gaze suddenly snapped to where they stood at the edge of the crowd. For a moment, her smile faltered, replaced by a flash of something hard and calculating. But then the mask was back in place, and she was once again the consummate showwoman, basking in the adulation of her audience.

As the final flames of her latest trick sputtered out and died, Beatrice Sands took a deep bow, her top hat sweeping the ground. The applause that followed was polite but somewhat muted, lacking the usual enthusiasm one might expect from a captivated audience.

Sands straightened, her smile faltering as she took in the crowd's lukewarm response. Whispers and murmurs rippled through the gathered onlookers, snatches of conversation reaching her ears.

"Where's Alex Meyer? He's usually here by now."

"I heard he's gone missing. Just vanished into thin air, they say."

"Probably just another one of his tricks. He'll turn up sooner or later."

Sands' jaw clenched, her eyes narrowing as she listened to the speculation about her rival's whereabouts. But she quickly smoothed her features into a mask of unconcern, waving off the mutters with a dismissive flick of her wrist.

"Thank you, thank you," she called out, her voice booming over the din. "You've been a wonderful audience. And remember, there's plenty more where that came from. Beatrice Sands is here to stay!"

With that, she jumped off the makeshift stage. Holmes and Watson followed in her wake, weaving through the dispersing crowd.

They caught up to Sands as she was packing away her props, her movements quick and jerky with barely suppressed anger. She looked up as they approached, her eyes flashing with annoyance.

"What do you want?" she snapped. "I'm busy."

"Miss Sands," Holmes said smoothly, inclining his head in greeting. "We were hoping to have a word with you about Mr Meyer."

At the mention of her rival's name, Sands' face twisted into a sneer. "What about him? The great Alex Meyer, vanished into thin air. Good riddance, I say."

Watson frowned, taken aback by the venom in her tone. "You don't seem overly concerned about his disappearance."

Sands snorted, shoving a handful of juggling balls into her bag with more force than necessary. "Why should I be? Meyer was nothing but a show-off, always hogging the limelight. He thought he was better than the rest of us, with his fancy tricks and big talk." She straightened, her eyes glittering with a hard, bitter light. "But look where it got him. Disappeared without a trace, and no one knows where he's gone. Well, I say it's about time someone else had a chance to shine."

Holmes studied her closely. "And you believe that someone should be you?"

Sands met his gaze defiantly, her chin jutting out. "Why not? I've got as much talent as Meyer ever did. More, even. And now that he's out of the picture, this patch is mine. And I'll fight anyone who tries to take it away from me."

Holmes asked, "Do you have any idea what might have happened to Mr Meyer? Any information you could provide would be most helpful."

Sands hesitated for a moment, appearing to wrestle with some internal debate.

"Well," she said at last, her voice grudging, "I suppose it's possible he's gone off to perform private shows for some toff who kept showing up to his performances. A man called Darlington, I think his name was."

Watson's eyebrows shot up in surprise. "Lord Hugh Darlington?" he asked, his voice incredulous.

Sands nodded. "That's the one. He often turned up here to watch Meyer. Seemed bewitched by him, he did. Like he'd never seen such a marvellous show before. He always had a chat with Meyer after the show. Getting along like great pals. Laughing, and then shaking hands as if agreeing to something." She stopped talking, looking left and right as though checking for eavesdroppers.

Holmes said, "There's something else you wish to say, Miss Sands? Something concerning Mr Meyer and Lord Darlington?"

Sands looked back at them. Her voice was lower as she said, "The night before Meyer disappeared, I saw him having a private discussion with Darlington. It was after his show. I couldn't hear what they were saying, but it looked intense. Like they were arguing about something. I noticed that Darlington didn't come back the following night. Perhaps they've fallen out about something."

Holmes nodded, his expression thoughtful. "Thank you, Miss Sands. You've been most helpful."

Sands gave them a curt nod, then turned back to her props, busying herself with packing them away.

Holmes and Watson walked away.

Watson said, "I presume we are going to pay a call on Lord Hugh Darlington."

Holmes smiled. "We are."

Chapter 5

Twenty minutes later, Holmes and Watson approached the imposing residence of Lord Hugh Darlington, which was situated in an affluent area of London.

Holmes knocked on the door, and once it was opened by a butler, Holmes made the necessary introductions and asked to speak to Lord Darlington.

The butler, a thin, severe-looking man, ushered them into the grand foyer with a disapproving sniff, his eyes narrowing as he took in their less-than-aristocratic attire.

"His Lordship will see you in the study," he said, barely concealing the disdain in his voice. "Follow me."

As they walked through the opulent halls, Watson marvelled at the sheer wealth on display. Priceless works of art adorned the walls, and the floors were covered in thick, plush carpets that muffled their footsteps. It was a far cry from the dingy streets of the East End.

The butler rapped sharply on the door of the study before opening it and announcing their presence. "Mr Sherlock Holmes and Dr John Watson to see you, my Lord."

Lord Darlington sat behind a massive mahogany desk, his steely grey eyes appraising them with a mixture of curiosity and contempt. He was every inch the aristocrat, from his perfectly tailored suit to the way he held himself with an air of entitled superiority.

"Mr Holmes, Dr Watson," he said, his voice smooth and cultured. "What is the nature of your visit?"

Holmes stepped forward. "We are investigating the disappearance of Alex Meyer, the street magician. We have reason to believe you may have information that could aid our inquiry."

Darlington raised an eyebrow. "And what makes you think I would have anything to do with a common street performer?"

Watson bristled at the dismissive tone, but Holmes remained unperturbed and said, "We have a witness account that places you at several of Mr Meyer's performances, as well as a private conversation between the two of you the night before he vanished. A somewhat heated conversation, it seems."

Darlington leaned back in his chair, regarding Holmes with a calculating gaze. "I won't deny I found the man's tricks mildly diverting. But as for any private conversations, I assure you, they were nothing more than idle chatter."

Holmes continued, "And yet, a mere street performer manages to capture the attention of a lord. Surely there must have been something more to your interest than idle curiosity."

Darlington's eyes flashed with anger, his jaw clenching tightly. "I don't like your tone, Mr Holmes. You forget yourself. I am not some common criminal to be interrogated. But I am willing to let you know why I was interested in Mr Meyer. His unique brand of entertainment had become quite the talk of the town, and I thought it would add a certain novelty to my social gatherings. So, after seeing his performances for myself, I engaged Mr Meyer's services for a series of exclusive soirees that took place here. I paid him well for his performances, very well indeed."

Watson asked, "And how did your guests take to Mr Meyer's presence?"

Darlington replied, "They were utterly enthralled, of course. The man may be uncouth and ill-bred, but there's no denying his skills border on the uncanny. Some even whispered that his tricks were impossible, that he must possess some sort of supernatural power."

"And what of your own opinion, Lord Darlington?" Holmes asked. "How did you find Mr Meyer's presence in your home?"

Darlington's posture stiffened, his shoulders squaring defensively. "I'll admit, the man was becoming overly familiar. I often saw him talking to the staff, which he had no business doing. It was unseemly. I had no choice but to terminate our arrangement on the night before he disappeared. He didn't take it well, but that's none of my concern."

"And do you have any idea where Mr Meyer might have gone?" Holmes asked.

Darlington shook his head, his expression turning cold and dismissive. "I haven't the faintest idea, nor do I care to speculate. As far as I'm concerned, the man is a liability, and I sincerely hope he never darkens the doorstep of my home again. One thing is certain, if the man ever returns, I will never again lower myself to watch another one of his shows. If that's all, Mr Holmes, you can take your leave now."

Chapter 6

After leaving Darlington's house, Holmes suggested they call on Mrs Meyer to let her know what they had uncovered so far.

"I only wish we had better news," he said to Watson. "But I'm certain we will discover what happened to Mr Meyer, no matter how long it takes."

Holmes and Watson headed through the streets in the direction of Mrs Meyer's modest abode. As they rounded the corner, they were met with an unexpected scene unfolding on the young woman's doorstep.

Samuel Burns, the journalist, loomed over Mrs Meyer, his rumpled form casting a shadow across her slight figure as she cradled a crying infant in her arms. His expression was one of intense determination, eyes alight with the scent of a story.

"Come now, Mrs Meyer," Burns implored, his tone a strange mixture of cajoling and insistence. "Surely you must be utterly heartbroken over your husband's disappearance. A few choice words from a devoted wife would add the right touch of anguish to my article."

Mrs Meyer's cheeks were flushed with distress. "Please, Mr Burns, I've told you all I know. Alex has simply vanished without a trace. I'm just as baffled as anyone."

Burns leaned in closer, his voice taking on a conspiratorial tone. "Or could it be, perhaps, that you know more than you're letting on? That you are behind his disappearance somehow. Maybe you were tired of living in your husband's shadow. Perhaps you saw your chance to become free of him, start again with someone new."

"How dare you!" Mrs Meyer gasped, clutching the squirming babe closer to her chest. "I would never do anything to harm my beloved Alex. He is my whole world."

Burns' eyes narrowed shrewdly as he regarded the flustered young woman. "Or perhaps this is all just an elaborate publicity stunt you and your husband cooked up together? After all, my research shows you were once his loyal assistant. You'd know all the tricks of his trade, wouldn't you?"

"Well, yes," she replied, her tone flustered. "I did assist Alex in his early days. But I would never dream of being part of some staged disappearance! I'm beside myself with worry over what's happened to him."

Burns hadn't finished with his interrogation. "Have you considered that your doting husband wanted to get out of this marriage and decided to do a vanishing act of his own accord? That he wanted to get away from the shackles of family life?"

"How dare you suggest such a thing!" the young woman cried out. "Alex loves me. He would never willingly abandon me and our child!"

At that moment, Holmes strode forward with purpose, his sharp eyes fixed on the journalist. "Mr Burns, that is quite enough," he said, interposing himself between the man and the distraught Mrs Meyer. "Your crass insinuations and badgering of this poor woman are entirely uncalled for. Kindly cease this interrogation at once."

Burns drew himself up to his full height, though he still had to crane his neck to meet the detective's steely gaze. "I'm only doing my job, Mr Holmes. There's a story to be had here, and I intend to be the one to write about it in the newspaper. The public has a right to know the truth about Alex Meyer's disappearance."

Holmes said, "The truth, Mr Burns? Or merely whatever sensationalised version of events will sell the most papers? I assure you, Dr Watson and I are more than capable of uncovering the facts of this case without your muckraking interference."

Burns' eyes glittered with a sly, calculating look. "And just how is your investigation progressing? I don't suppose you've managed to find out about Alex Meyer's secret deal with Lord Darlington, have you?"

Mrs Meyer let out a gasp of surprise. "What? Alex, involved with Lord Darlington? I don't understand. Mr Holmes, what does he mean? Is that true?"

Before Holmes could answer, Burns said, "There was definitely something going on between them. I wouldn't be surprised if Darlington had something to do with your husband's disappearance. I'm going to find out the truth, just you wait and see."

With a final mocking laugh, Burns turned around and sauntered away.

Holmes turned his attention to Mrs Meyer, his expression softening as he took in her distressed state. "Might we trouble you for a private word about our investigation thus far? I believe it would be most beneficial to discuss matters in a more discreet setting."

The young woman nodded, her eyes still brimming with unshed tears. "Of course. Please, do come inside." She stepped back from the doorway, beckoning for the two men to follow her into the house.

As they crossed the threshold, Holmes took in the tidy, well-kept interior of the house. Despite the young couple's humble circumstances, it was clear that Mrs Meyer took great pride in maintaining a clean and comfortable home. The floors were swept, the furniture dusted, and cheerful sprigs of wildflowers adorned the mantelpiece and windowsills.

The only thing marring the tranquil scene was the continued fussing of the baby in Mrs Meyer's arms. The infant's face was scrunched up in distress, his cries growing more insistent by the moment.

"May I?" Dr Watson asked, holding out his arms towards the squirming bundle. "Perhaps I could try to soothe the little chap while you and Holmes discuss matters."

Mrs Meyer replied, "Thank you, Dr Watson. I would appreciate that very much."

Carefully, she transferred the fussing infant into Watson's waiting arms. The doctor cradled the child close to his chest, murmuring soothing nonsense words as he began to rock back and forth in a gentle, swaying motion. Gradually, the baby's cries began to quiet, his eyelids drooping as he succumbed to the lulling rhythm of Watson's movements.

Holmes watched the interaction with a small smile before turning his attention back to the young woman. "Now then, Mrs Meyer, let us discuss what we have learned thus far about your husband's disappearance. I must warn you, however, that some of the information we have uncovered may be difficult for you to hear."

Mrs Meyer nodded. "I understand, Mr Holmes. But I must know the truth, no matter how painful it may be."

Chapter 7

Mrs Meyer settled herself on the worn but comfortable settee, her hands clasped tightly in her lap. Watson continued to sway gently with the now-sleeping baby in his arms, his attention divided between the child and the unfolding conversation.

Holmes took a seat opposite and said, "Mrs Meyer, I'm afraid that Mr Burns was right about your husband's connection with Lord Darlington. He had been performing private shows for Lord Darlington and his society friends at his lordship's residence."

Mrs Meyer's brow furrowed. "Private shows? For Lord Darlington? But Alex never mentioned anything of the sort to me."

Holmes continued, "It seems that your husband had been supplementing his income with these exclusive performances. Lord Darlington himself confirmed as much during our visit to his home."

Mrs Meyer shook her head. "I don't understand why he wouldn't have told me. I mean, yes, he had been bringing in more money lately, but I just assumed it was because his street show was doing so well. I never imagined..." She trailed off as the implications of Holmes' words sank in. "If he kept the truth from me about that, what else has he been hiding? I thought we shared everything, Mr Holmes. I thought I knew my husband."

"I know this must be a terrible shock," Holmes said. "But I promise you, we will get to the bottom of this mystery and discover the truth about your husband's disappearance. You have my word on that."

"Thank you. I feel so lost and confused right now. I don't know what to think or who to trust."

"I understand," Holmes said. "Mrs Meyer, I overheard Mr Burns mentioning something about your time as an assistant to your husband. Could you tell us more about that?"

Despite her distress, the young woman smiled. "Those were such happy times. We met about eight years ago. I was just a girl then, barely sixteen and fresh off the train from the country. I stumbled across Alex quite by accident one day, performing his magic in a crowded square. I was utterly enchanted by his skill and showmanship, and I couldn't help but linger to watch. He must have noticed me, because after the show, he approached me and struck up a conversation.

"We talked for hours that day, about everything and nothing at all. He offered me a job as his assistant. He said he could see something special in me, a spark of potential just waiting to be ignited. And oh, Mr Holmes, I was so thrilled at the prospect! To be a part of something so exciting and glamorous, to work alongside such a brilliant and charismatic man. It seemed like a dream come true."

She paused, her expression turning soft as she lost herself cherished memories. "Those early days were some of the happiest of my life. Learning the tricks of the trade from Alex, watching him captivate audiences with his magic night after night. It was like being a part of something truly special. And somewhere along the way, amidst all the laughter and the wonder and the long hours spent perfecting our craft, I fell head over heels in love with him. And miracle of miracles, he fell in love with me too."

Holmes smiled at the woman. "May I ask, during your time as an assistant, did you become familiar with the trick involving the trunk? The trick he performed last night. Do you know how it works?"

A flicker of unease crossed Mrs Meyer's face. "Yes, I know how it works. Alex and I developed it together. It was meant to be the grand finale of his show, the one that would leave audiences truly astounded."

Holmes said, "Dr Watson and I examined the trunk earlier and discovered that the back panel comes down when pressed in a certain place. Is that part of the trick, too?"

Mrs Meyer shook her head. "No, but Alex had that panel installed for future tricks he was planning." She abruptly stopped talking. Her eyes widened. "Mr Holmes, do you think someone knew about that back panel and forced Alex out of the trunk using it? That would explain how he disappeared. But who would do such a thing? And why would Alex allow that to happen without putting up a fight?"

Holmes said, "It's possible he was forced out. Mrs Meyer, can we discuss your husband's assistant again? Are you aware of any grudges between your husband and Mr Turner? Any jealousies, any disputes?"

Mrs Meyer replied, "No, nothing comes to mind. Alex and Jack seemed to get along well enough. Jack was always eager to learn from Alex. And Alex seemed to enjoy teaching him, moulding him into a proper magician's assistant. Do you think Jack is involved somehow?"

Holmes said, "We have to consider every possibility." He glanced over at Watson, who was still gently cradling the sleeping baby in his arms. "I think perhaps it's time we paid a visit to Mr Turner. Do you have his address, Mrs Meyer?"

"Yes, I do. He lives in a boarding house not far from here, just a few streets over."

She rattled off the address, which Holmes dutifully jotted down in his notebook. Then, with a final reassuring smile for Mrs Meyer, he rose to his feet.

"Thank you again for your time and cooperation," Holmes said, inclining his head respectfully. "I promise you, we will do everything in our power to find your husband."

Watson carefully transferred the still-sleeping baby to his crib, taking care not to jostle him. Then, with a final nod of farewell to the young woman, the two men left the house, stepping out into the bustling London street with renewed determination to solve the mystery of Alex Meyer's disappearance.

Chapter 8

It wasn't long before Holmes and Watson arrived at the modest boarding house where Mr Turner resided, a nondescript building nestled among a row of similar dwellings.

They climbed the narrow stairs to the second floor, the wooden boards creaking beneath their feet. Holmes rapped sharply on the door of Turner's room.

After a moment, the door swung open to reveal a young man with a shock of sandy hair and a face etched with worry. His eyes widened as he took in the imposing figure of Sherlock Holmes standing before him.

"Mr Turner?" Holmes inquired, his voice crisp and businesslike. "I am Sherlock Holmes, and this is Dr Watson. We are investigating the disappearance of Alex Meyer, and we were hoping you might be able to shed some light on the matter."

The young man stepped back to allow the two men entry into his small, sparsely furnished room. "Of course," he said. "Come in."

Holmes and Watson settled themselves on the room's only two chairs, while Turner perched on the edge of his narrow bed.

Holmes began, "Mrs Meyer tells us that you were assisting Alex with his performance on the night he disappeared. Can you tell us exactly what happened?"

Turner nodded, swallowing hard. "Yes, of course. Everything was going as planned. Alex had performed the trick flawlessly dozens of times before. I would tie him up and help him into the trunk. Alex would then escape from his chains and reappear moments later. But last night, something went wrong. Alex had got into the trunk, all tied up, and I closed the lid as I always do. But then, a child in the audience started crying. Really loudly. He was making such a noise that everyone turned around to look at him. Including me.

"I didn't want anything to ruin Alex's triumphant escape from the trunk, so I ran over to the boy and asked him what the matter was. He said he was worried about the magician going into the box and never coming out again.

I tried my best to calm him down, and so did other people around him."

Holmes interrupted, "Did the child have any parents or guardians with him?"

"Not that I noticed," Turner replied. "It took me a minute or so to calm him down. I kept looking back at the trunk, expecting Alex to reappear. But as the seconds went by, I started to get an uneasy feeling. I ran back to the trunk, and tapped lightly on it, expecting Alex to tap back. This was our secret code in case anything ever went wrong with the trick. But there was no return tap, so I opened the trunk, and, well, it was empty. Alex had gone. And it's all my fault. If I had just kept my attention on the trick, this wouldn't have happened." He shook his head in dismay.

Watson said, "You mustn't blame yourself, Mr Turner. You were only trying to help a frightened child. No one could fault you for that."

Holmes added his opinion. "It's possible the crying child was part of a plan to remove Mr Meyer from the trunk. The child caused a disturbance, which allowed you to become distracted long enough for Mr Meyer to be removed from the trunk. Which means that whoever did this, knew Mr Meyer's trick well. They also knew about the trunk's hidden exit. Mr Turner, can you think of anyone who might have wanted Mr Meyer out of the way? Anyone who might have had reason to wish him harm?"

"Well," Turner began, his voice hesitant. "There is one person who comes to mind. Beatrice Sands, another street performer who's been working in that area for years. She's always been jealous of Alex's success, always resented the way he seemed to draw in the crowds while she struggled to make ends meet."

Holmes nodded. "Yes, we are aware of Miss Sand's feelings towards Mr Meyer and have already spoken to her about his disappearance. What about Lord Darlington? Did you know about Mr Meyer's agreement to perform at his home?"

Turner shook his head. "No, I had no idea. I saw them talking to each other sometimes after the show, but Alex never said anything about private performances."

Watson asked, "But why would he keep something like that from you? Surely he would have wanted you by his side at Lord Darlington's house, helping him to put on the best possible performance?"

Turner's face fell. "I don't know. Maybe he didn't trust me. Maybe he thought I wasn't good enough to perform for the likes of Lord Darlington." He shook his head, trying to make sense of it all.

Holmes asked, "Did you see Mr Meyer talking to Lord Darlington on the night before he went missing?"

"Yes, now that you mention it, I do remember seeing them together that night. It looked like they were having an argument. I couldn't hear what they were saying, but it ended with Darlington storming off."

"Thank you for your help," Holmes said, rising from the chair. "If you think of anything else that might help, do contact us."

Turner nodded. "I will. I hope you find Alex soon."

With that, Holmes and Watson left the building and walked along the street, lost in discussion about what Turner had told them. They had barely taken a dozen steps, however, when a familiar figure caught their eye.

Beatrice Sands was striding towards them, a broad grin on her face. She was dressed in her usual flamboyant attire, a garish mix of bright colours and clashing patterns that seemed designed to draw the eye and hold it captive.

As she drew near, Beatrice raised a hand in greeting, her voice booming out across the crowded street. "Mr Holmes! Dr Watson! What a pleasant surprise to see you here. I don't suppose you've had any luck finding our dear Alex, have you?"

Holmes regarded her coolly, his expression giving nothing away. "I'm afraid not, Miss Sands. The investigation is still ongoing, and we have yet to uncover any concrete leads as to his whereabouts."

To Watson's surprise, the woman's grin only widened at this news, her eyes sparkling with barely contained glee. "Well, that is a shame," she said, her voice dripping with false sympathy. "But I suppose it's to be expected. But with Alex out of the picture, I can take over his spot permanently. I've got plans, big plans to create a show so dazzling, so mind-boggling, that the crowds will forget Alex Meyer ever existed. And to do that, I'm going to need an assistant. Someone young, someone eager, someone who knows the ins and outs of the business. Someone like Jack Turner."

Holmes' eyes narrowed. "And what makes you think Mr Turner would be willing to work with you, Miss Sands? He seems quite loyal to Mr Meyer, and deeply concerned about his disappearance."

Sands waved a dismissive hand, her expression one of supreme confidence. "Oh, I have my ways, Mr Holmes. I can be very persuasive when I want to be. And let's face it, with Alex gone, Jack's going to need a new job. I'm sure I can convince him to forget all about his old boss and join forces with me instead. Just you wait and see. In a few weeks' time, the name on everyone's lips won't be Alex Meyer. It'll be Beatrice Sands, the greatest street magician London has ever seen."

Chapter 9

As the night was drawing in, Holmes and Watson returned to their lodgings at 221B Baker Street. After a hearty meal, they settled into their armchairs and began to discuss their latest investigation.

"It seems to me, Watson," Holmes began, "that our primary suspects at this juncture are Beatrice Sands and Jack Turner."

Watson nodded. "Yes, I can see why you'd think that. Sands certainly has the motive to want Alex out of the picture. With him gone, she could easily step in and take over his act."

"Precisely," Holmes agreed. "And as a fellow magician, she would have the knowledge and expertise to know exactly how the trunk trick works and when Mr Meyer would be free of his chains. It's not outside the realm of possibility that she could have orchestrated Alex's disappearance during the performance. She could have also organised for that child to make enough of a fuss to distract Mr Turner for long enough to make her move."

"But how would she have managed it?" Watson asked. "Surely Mr Meyer would have called out if she had tried to remove him from the trunk."

"Indeed, he might have. But we must consider the possibility that Sands found a way to silence him. She may have used brute force, or have been armed with some sort of weapon."

"Good lord, Holmes. You don't really think she would have gone that far, do you?"

Holmes replied, "There's a reason why Mr Meyer left the trunk silently, and having a weapon aimed at him, would certainly achieve that. But Miss Sands is not our only suspect. Now, let's discuss Jack Turner. It's possible he knew more about Mr Meyer's secret work with Lord Darlington than he let on. Perhaps he was jealous of the attention and opportunities that Mr Meyer was receiving. With his employer now out of the way, Mr Turner is in a position to offer his services to Lord Darlington."

Watson leaned back in his chair. "But how would Mr Turner have done it?"

"He could have enlisted the help of someone," Holmes answered. "Perhaps Miss Sands. They could have worked together to remove Mr Meyer. And you heard Miss Sand's boasts about taking over his spot and how she's now planning on having Mr Turner as her assistant."

Watson sighed. "It's a lot to consider."

Holmes said, "There is, of course, someone else who knows about the trunk's hidden exit, and she knows how the trick works."

Watson sat up straighter. "Surely you don't mean Mrs Meyer? But why on earth would she want to harm her own husband?"

"Maybe their marriage was not as idyllic as she would have us believe. Perhaps Alex Meyer was having an affair, and she discovered his infidelity. Or maybe Mrs Meyer had grown tired of living in his shadow, just like Samuel Burns claimed."

Watson nodded slowly, considering the idea. "But she seemed genuinely distraught when she came to us for help. Surely if she is behind her husband's disappearance, she would have been more composed?"

"Ah, but that's just it, Watson," Holmes replied, a glint in his eye. "Mrs Meyer is a performer herself, remember? She knows how to put on a convincing show."

Watson nodded. "Before we attempt the task of proving any of these theories, do you have any other suspects in mind?"

"Only Lord Darlington and Mr Burns, our not-so-friendly local journalist. Mr Burns for the fame, of course. Kidnapping Mr Meyer and then releasing him a few days later would make an unforgettable piece in his newspaper. As for Lord Darlington, there is something he's hiding. I would like to know what his public disagreement with Mr Meyer was really about."

Watson attempted to stifle a yawn, but failed. "I do apologise, Holmes. It's been a busy day, and there is a lot to consider in this latest investigation."

"I agree," Holmes said. "I'll write my thoughts down and see if I can make any sense of them. Then, tomorrow, we will start afresh with clear minds. Why don't you get an early night, Watson?"

The good doctor rose from his chair. "Excellent idea. I'll do that. Goodnight, Holmes. Don't stay up too late."

"I won't," Holmes replied, his thoughts already back on the perplexing case of the vanishing magician.

Chapter 10

The following morning, Holmes and Watson returned to Fleet Street to talk to Samuel Burns again. Holmes was convinced the journalist knew more than he was letting on, and Holmes was determined to find out what that was.

As they entered the newspaper's office, however, it was immediately apparent that something was amiss. The usual bustle and energy of the newsroom was subdued, replaced by an atmosphere of worry and concern. It was soon apparent that Burns wasn't in the office.

Holmes approached one of the other reporters, a young man with a harried expression. "Excuse me, but where is Mr Burns? We have some questions for him regarding a story he's been working on."

The reporter looked up, his face drawn. "Burns hasn't been seen since yesterday. He was supposed to meet us at the pub as usual last night, but he never showed. And now he hasn't turned up for work, which is unusual for him."

Watson asked, "Has anyone checked his home? Perhaps he's been taken ill."

The reporter replied, "One of my colleagues called round there this morning, but there was no answer. It's not like Burns to disappear like this."

Holmes asked, "What was Mr Burns working on when he was last here? Any particular stories or leads?"

The reporter hesitated, glancing around the newsroom before leaning in closer. "Burns was always secretive about his work, especially when he thought he had a big scoop. But he seemed particularly pleased with himself yesterday, said he'd uncovered a new lead that would blow the lid off something big."

"Did he happen to mention Lord Darlington at all?" Holmes said, his tone casual but his gaze sharp.

The reporter let out a bitter laugh. "Darlington? Everyone in the newspaper business knows that man is as corrupt as they come. But no one's ever been able to prove it. He's too well-connected, too powerful. He'll never be brought to justice. The truth will never be revealed."

Holmes nodded, his expression thoughtful as he regarded the man. He moved over to Burns' desk, Watson following close behind. They began to sift through the scattered papers and notebooks, looking for anything that might provide a clue to the journalist's disappearance.

"Holmes, look at this," Watson said, holding up a scrap of paper with a hastily scribbled address on it. "It looks like a country estate of some kind."

Holmes took the paper, studying it closely. He showed it to the reporter. "Do you recognise this address?"

The reporter said, "That's Darlington's country house. But why would Burns have written that down?"

"An excellent question," Holmes said, memorising the address on the note. He thanked the reporter for his help and returned the slip of paper to the desk.

Holmes and Watson left the building and stopped on the pavement outside it.

"Where should we go now?" Watson asked. "Shall we question some of our suspects again?"

Holmes said, "The disappearance of Mr Burns has added a new layer of complexity to our case. I wonder if he went to Lord Darlington's estate yesterday."

The detective's keen eyes scanned the row of waiting hansom cabs, and he strode purposefully towards the drivers.

"Gentlemen," Holmes called out, his voice carrying above the din of the street. "I'm looking for the driver who possibly took a passenger to Lord Darlington's country estate yesterday. A journalist by the name of Samuel Burns."

The drivers exchanged glances, until one of them, a grizzled man with a weather-beaten face, spoke up. "Aye, that was me. I remember that chap, talked my ear off the whole way there."

Holmes and Watson approached the driver.

"Did Mr Burns mention why he was going there?" Holmes asked.

The driver let out a hearty laugh,shaking his head. "Oh, he wouldn't shut up about it. Kept going on about this big scoop he was landing for his paper. Something about a street magician and a well-known man in high society. He was mighty boastful about the whole thing. Kept saying how this story was going to make his career, put him on the map, it would."

Holmes said, "What happened when you arrived at the estate? Did Mr Burns ask you to wait for him?"

The driver said, "No, he didn't. I offered, but he said there was no need. Said he'd find his own way back."

Holmes turned to Watson, lowering his voice. "Mr Burns may have stumbled onto something bigger than he realised. Something that connects Alex Meyer's disappearance to Lord Darlington. We need to get to Lord Darlington's estate and see if Mr Burns is still there. If he had uncovered something big, he would have returned to his office immediately to type up his article. The fact that he hasn't done that, is a worry. Perhaps he's being held at the estate against his will."

Watson nodded. "Yes, that is possible."

Holmes' attention was suddenly caught by someone hurrying out of the newspaper office. He gave them a curious glance, but didn't say anything to Watson.

Holmes asked the cab driver to take them to Lord Darlington's country estate, and to make a short detour on the way there.

The two men climbed into the hansom cab. The driver cracked his whip, and the horse set off at a brisk trot.

At Holmes' request, the cab stopped a few minutes later. Holmes leapt out of the cab and raced into a building. He returned shortly and got back into the cab, telling Watson his task had been completed and they were ready to proceed. Watson didn't ask any questions, having complete faith in Holmes that his task was related to their investigation somehow.

Chapter 11

The hansom cab rattled along the cobblestone streets, carrying Holmes and Watson away from the bustling heart of London. As the city's dense sprawl gave way to the rolling countryside, the landscape transformed before their eyes. Lush green fields stretched out on either side of the road, dotted with grazing sheep and the occasional farmhouse. The air grew crisp and clean, carrying the scent of wildflowers and freshly cut hay.

Less than an hour later, the cab turned onto a long, winding driveway lined with towering oak trees. At the end of the drive stood the impressive country estate of Lord Darlington, a grand Georgian mansion with sprawling gardens and immaculate lawns. As they drew closer, it became apparent that the estate was closed. The windows were shuttered, and the gardens showed signs of neglect, with overgrown hedges and untended flowerbeds.

Holmes paid the driver and exchanged a few quiet words with him. The driver nodded in understanding before turning his horse around and heading back down the driveway. As the sound of the cab's wheels faded into the distance, Holmes and Watson approached the main entrance of the mansion.

The detective rapped sharply on the heavy wooden door, but no answer came. He tried the handle, but it was locked. Undeterred, Holmes began to examine the ground around the entrance, his keen eyes scanning for any signs of recent activity.

"Watson, look here," he said, pointing to a disturbance in the gravel driveway. "Someone has been here recently. The rest of the gravel is smooth and undisturbed, but this area shows signs of activity."

Watson crouched down to examine the marks. "Do you think it could be Mr Burns? Perhaps he found a way inside to search for whatever evidence he was after."

Holmes nodded. "Mr Burns is a tenacious journalist, and he wouldn't let a locked door stop him from pursuing a story. We need to find a way inside as well."

Holmes and Watson circled the perimeter of the grand estate, scanning every nook and cranny for signs of entry. The detective's keen gaze soon fell upon a glint of something amidst the overgrown shrubbery. He moved closer, pushing aside the tangled vines to reveal a broken window, its jagged edges catching the sunlight. Fragments of cloth were caught on the broken glass.

"Aha!" Holmes exclaimed. "It appears our intrepid journalist found his way inside after all. The torn edges of his coat suggest he entered through this very window. We must follow him."

Watson peered through the opening. "It's a tight squeeze, Holmes. Are you certain we should follow the same path?"

"Needs must, my dear Watson," Holmes replied, already shrugging off his coat and rolling up his sleeves. He used his coat to push the remaining shards of glass into the room beyond. "We must hurry. Mr Burns could be in danger."

With a grunt of effort, Holmes hoisted himself up and through the broken window, landing lightly on his feet inside. Watson followed suit, his larger frame requiring a bit more manoeuvring to navigate the narrow opening.

They were in a dimly lit storeroom, its shelves lined with dusty bottles and crates. The air was stale and musty, tinged with the faint scent of mildew.

Holmes scanned the room, looking for any signs of the journalist, or clues. He found neither and told Watson they should search the rest of the building.

As they made their way towards the door, a muffled sound caught their attention. It was faint, barely audible above the creaking of the old floorboards beneath their feet.

"Did you hear that?" Holmes whispered. "It seems to be coming from below us."

The two men crept out of the storeroom and into the main hallway of the mansion. The sound grew louder still, a muffled thumping rising from beneath them.

"There must be a cellar," Holmes noted. "But where is the door to it?"

They searched the hallway before them until they found a door that was marked as the cellar.

Holmes reached for the handle. But the door was locked, its iron bolt firmly in place.

Undeterred, Holmes reached into his jacket and produced a set of slender tools. With deft movements, he set to work on the lock. Seconds later, there was a satisfying click, and the door swung open.

Holmes and Watson descended the narrow stone steps into the cellar, their eyes straining to adjust to the dim light that filtered through a small, high window. The thumping sound was louder now, more insistent, as if someone was pounding on the floor or wall. As they moved deeper into the room, their hearts raced with anticipation, wondering what, or rather who, they would find ahead.

Chapter 12

There, against the far wall, they saw two figures. Both were bound and gagged. Holmes rushed forward, immediately recognising the dishevelled forms of Alex Meyer and Samuel Burns. Meyer's once-dazzling stage outfit was torn and dirty, his face pale and drawn. Burns, on the other hand, was red-faced and struggling against his bonds, his eyes blazing with indignation.

Holmes quickly untied the cloth around Meyer's mouth, allowing the magician to take a deep, shuddering breath. "Are you alright, Mr Meyer?" the detective asked.

Meyer nodded. "Yes, I think so. But my wife, my child, are they safe?"

"They are," Watson reassured him, already working on the ropes that bound the magician's wrists.

Burns, however, was not so easily placated. As soon as his gag was removed, he launched into a tirade, his voice echoing off the stone walls. "It's about time you showed up, Holmes! What took you so long to find me? Call yourself a detective! When we get out of here, don't you forget it was me who figured out where Meyer was, not you! I knew his disappearance was linked to Darlington, and that it was something to do with his lordship's unscrupulous dealings. And I've got evidence, I tell you. Evidence that will bring down that pompous Darlington and expose his corrupt dealings once and for all! This is my story, not yours!"

Meyer winced as he rubbed his chafed wrists. "For the love of God, Holmes, can you please shut him up? Can you put that gag back? I know what he's like. He'll never shut up now that he's free to talk."

Holmes and Watson exchanged a glance, the detective's eyes glinting with amusement. "Perhaps we should focus on getting you both out of here first," Holmes suggested. "Then we can discuss the finer points of who deserves credit for what."

As Holmes leaned in to untie the muttering Burns, a voice behind him cut through the silence of the cellar.

"Well, well, well. What have we here?" Lord Darlington stood at the foot of the stairs, flanked by a group of burly men holding guns. His eyes glinted with a dangerous light as he surveyed the scene before him. "It seems I'll have to dispose of four bodies now, not just one. Such a pity, really. I had hoped to keep this mess contained."

"Now look here!" Watson cried out, taking a step closer to Darlington. Holmes put his hand out and stopped Watson from taking another step.

Darlington turned his gaze to Meyer, who met it with a defiant glare. "This is all your fault, you know," Darlington said, his tone turning icy. "If you had just kept your end of the bargain and continued those private performances at my house, none of this would have happened."

Meyer lifted his chin. "I couldn't do it anymore. Not after I discovered the true nature of your illegal activities. I couldn't mix with the likes of you and your friends. And I certainly couldn't take your money any longer, not after I knew where it was coming from. I know you've always looked down on me, treating me like a performing monkey, but I still have a moral compass."

Darlington let out a harsh laugh. "Morality? How quaint. Look where your precious morals have got you, Meyer. Tied up in a cellar, along with your meddling journalist friend and the famous Sherlock Holmes and Dr Watson."

Meyer shot Holmes an apologetic look. Holmes responded by giving him an almost imperceptible shake of his head.

Darlington glowered at the magician. "Their deaths will be on your hands, Meyer. You brought this upon them with your foolish idealism."

Meyer's face paled, but he refused to back down. "Not everyone is as corrupt as you and your associates. There are still good people in this world, people who will fight against the likes of you."

Darlington turned to his men, jerking his head towards the captives. "Tie them up. And make sure they're secure this time. We can't have them escaping before the grand finale."

The burly men moved forward, their guns trained on the helpless captives. Ropes were tied around the prisoners, but to Holmes' relief, no gags were used.

Once the ropes were firmly in place, Darlington stood before them. He said, "I have pressing business to attend to in London. But fear not. I shall return soon enough to put an end to your miserable lives. Do try to make yourselves comfortable in the meantime. Not that it will matter much in the end."

With a final, mocking laugh, Darlington left the cellar, his men following close behind. The heavy door slammed shut, the sound of the lock clicking into place echoing through the confined space.

Burns let out a hollow laugh, shaking his head. "I never should have got involved in this. All I wanted was a good story, something to make my name in the papers. And now look at me. Tied up in a cellar, waiting for death. I hope my obituary will be a good one."

But Holmes, ever the calm and collected figure, refused to succumb to despair. "Do not give up hope just yet, Mr Burns. I already have a plan in place, one that will see us out of this predicament and bring Lord Darlington to justice."

Meyer and Burns looked at the detective in surprise and scepticism, but Watson knew better than to doubt his friend. He smiled and waited for Holmes to reveal his plan.

Chapter 13

Despite Holmes' reassurance that they would soon be out, Burns continued to moan about their situation and filled the silence with one grumble after another.

Holmes ignored the journalist, turned his attention to Meyer, and asked, "Why did you not free yourself from your ties and escape this cellar when you were first brought here? Surely a man of your talents could have managed such a feat."

Meyer sighed heavily. "I could have, Mr Holmes. But Darlington threatened to hurt my wife and child if I attempted to escape. I couldn't risk their safety. I would rather die than see any harm come to my family."

Holmes nodded, his expression one of understanding. "And how did you come to be taken from the trunk during your performance?"

"It was Beatrice Sands," Meyer replied. "Do you know who she is?"

Holmes inclined his head. "Yes, we have met Miss Sands."

Meyer continued, "Beatrice had been paid by Darlington to kidnap me. She took me by surprise when she opened the back of the trunk just as I had removed the last of my shackles. She instantly warned me that if I made a sound, my family would suffer the consequences. So I kept silent, allowing myself to be dragged out of the trunk."

Watson shook his head. "What a despicable thing to do, and to a fellow magician, too."

Holmes said, "Mr Meyer, rest assured, your family is now safe. No harm will come to them, I guarantee that. In which case, you are now free to untie yourself. Would you be so kind to untie Mr Burns and Dr Watson as well? You will note that I have already freed myself." He held up his hands.

Meyer looked at Holmes in surprise. "How did you...?" he began, but Holmes merely smiled.

"A detective never reveals his secrets," Holmes said, his tone light despite the gravity of their situation. "But suffice it to say, I have a few tricks up my sleeve as well."

Meyer set to work, releasing first himself, and then Burns and Watson.

Once the men were free, Burns dashed towards the cellar steps and yelled, "Come on, quick! Before they come back!"

Holmes called, "There's no need to rush, Mr Burns. The police will already be outside, and with any luck, they will have apprehended Lord Darlington by now."

Burns stopped in his tracks and looked over his shoulder. "What do you mean? How could the police be here?"

Holmes explained, "When Dr Watson and I visited Fleet Street earlier, we had a rather enlightening conversation with one of your fellow reporters. He seemed quite convinced that Lord Darlington would never be caught, but there was something about his demeanour that struck me as insincere."

Watson nodded. "Yes, I remember that. The chap seemed a bit too eager to dismiss the idea of Darlington facing justice."

"Precisely," Holmes agreed. "And when we stepped outside to hail a cab, I noticed the very same reporter dashing off in the direction of Darlington's residence, no doubt intent on warning him of our investigation and that we had discovered the address of his country estate. On the way here, I took the precaution of letting one of my contacts at the police station know where we were heading and why.

I told him that I suspected Lord Darlington was holding Mr Meyer and Mr Burns captive. The officer advised the police have been after Lord Darlington for years, and they would head to the estate immediately."

Burns shook his head in disbelief, a grudging respect in his voice. "But how could you have been so certain that your assumption was correct, Mr Holmes? It seems like an awful lot to hang on a mere hunch."

Holmes replied, "My dear Mr Burns, I am always right." He paused for a moment, his smile widening. "Well, almost always. Let us go outside and see if the police have detained Lord Darlington and his associates."

"And if they haven't?" Burns couldn't help asking. "What if he's got away like he always does?"

"I doubt that is the case this time, Mr Burns," Holmes replied. "But if such an unlikely event has occurred, then we will deal with it. I assure you, Lord Darlington will not evade an arrest, not if I've got anything to do with it."

"Hmmph," came Burns' reply. He ascended the steps and reached for the door handle. He attempted to twist it. "Well, we're not going to get very far, are we, with the door being locked!"

Holmes calmly replied, "It won't be locked for long." He looked at Mr Meyer, raised one eyebrow and asked, "Would you like to open it, or shall I?"

Meyer smiled. "Let me. I've been dreaming about opening it since the second I was brought in here."

With deft movements, the experienced magician opened the door, and the four men stepped out of the dismal cellar.

Holmes took the lead and strode ahead. "Let us exit this building, gentlemen. We wouldn't want to miss the look of defeat on Darlington's face."

"Indeed," Watson replied. "Lead on, Holmes."

Burns muttered under his breath to Meyer, "I'm almost hoping Holmes is wrong. That'll wipe the smug look off his face."

Meyer shook his head. "You really are the most annoying man, Mr Burns."

Chapter 14

The four men stepped out of the house and into the bright sunlight. A scene of controlled chaos greeted them. The sprawling grounds of Darlington's estate were swarming with police officers, their dark uniforms a stark contrast against the manicured lawns.

In the centre of the commotion, Lord Darlington stood, his face a mask of fury and indignation as two officers held him firmly by the arms. His once immaculate attire was now dishevelled, his hair falling into his eyes as he struggled against the grip of the law.

"Unhand me at once!" Darlington bellowed, his voice carrying across the grounds. "This is an outrage! I demand to speak to your superior officer immediately!"

One of the officers, a stout man with a bushy moustache, merely tightened his hold on the enraged aristocrat. "I'm afraid that won't be possible, your lordship," he said, his tone firm but respectful. "You're under arrest for the kidnapping of Mr Alex Meyer and Mr Samuel Burns."

Darlington's eyes widened, his face turning an alarming shade of purple. "Kidnapping? This is preposterous! I have done no such thing!"

Holmes moved forward and said, "I beg to differ, Lord Darlington. As you can see, I have managed to escape from the bounds you placed upon me. I'm sure there is ample evidence to prove your involvement in the abduction of Mr Burns and Mr Meyer, along with the detainment of myself and Dr Watson."

Darlington sputtered, "You have no idea who you're dealing with, Mr Holmes. I have friends in high places. You will never prove anything!"

Burns, who had been watching the exchange with barely contained glee, suddenly dashed forward, waving a sheaf of papers in the air. "I wouldn't be so sure about that, your lordship," he crowed, his eyes glinting with triumph. "I've got evidence here that proves your involvement in all sorts of corrupt dealings. Bribery, blackmail, you name it!"

Darlington yelled, "Where did you get those? Those are private documents."

Burns grinned. "Let's just say I have my sources. And I think the police will be very interested in what these papers have to say."

The officers led Darlington away. The aristocrat's shoulders slumped, the fight draining out of him as the reality of his situation sank in.

Meyer, who had been watching the scene unfold, turned to Holmes and said, "I can't thank you enough. You've saved my life."

Holmes replied, "I only wish we could have intervened sooner. Now, let's get you back to your family, shall we?"

Meyer nodded. "Do you think I should ask the police for a lift in one of their cabs? I feel a bit embarrassed doing so, though."

Holmes said, "There's no need for that, Mr Meyer. I asked the cab driver who brought us here to wait for us, but to hide himself when Darlington's cab showed up."

As if on cue, the cab approached, the smiling driver raising a hand at the detective.

The cab came to a stop, and Holmes, Watson, and Meyer climbed inside.

Burns gave Holmes a sheepish look and asked if he could have a lift.

Holmes replied, "Only if you promise to stay silent on the journey."

The journalist opened his mouth, ready to complain, but wisely closed it and climbed into the cab.

Chapter 15

A few days later, Holmes and Watson were enjoying a quiet morning at 221B Baker Street. Watson, ensconced in his favourite armchair, was engrossed in the day's newspaper when he suddenly exclaimed in surprise.

"I say, Holmes, listen to this! Lord Darlington has confessed to all the charges raised against him, including kidnapping and corrupt dealings."

Holmes, who had been languidly smoking his pipe, merely raised an eyebrow. "I suspect he was offered a deal to secure his confession. No doubt there will be some benefit to him in exchange for his cooperation."

Watson read on. "It seems Darlington has named those who were in dealings with him and benefitted from his illegal activities. And he's also identified Beatrice Sands as an accomplice in Alex Meyer's abduction." He lowered the paper. "What I don't understand is why Miss Sands pointed us in the direction of Lord Darlington when we first met her. Considering her involvement in the kidnapping, it would have been wiser for her to keep quiet about him."

Holmes said, "Miss Sands was confident that Lord Darlington would get away with his crime, as he always does. Also, misdirection is part of a magician's expertise. She aimed the blame at Lord Darlington and away from herself. Perhaps safe in the knowledge that Darlington would never be brought to justice."

Watson nodded. He smiled and said, "It was truly wonderful to see Mr Meyer reunited with his wife and child."

"I agree, Watson. It was a satisfying conclusion to a most intriguing case."

As the morning wore on, the conversation turned to other matters - the latest developments in the world of science, the state of affairs in the British Empire, and the ever-present possibility of a new mystery waiting just around the corner.

For now, however, Holmes and Watson were content to savour the moment of peace and camaraderie, secure in the knowledge that whatever challenges lay ahead, they would face them together, as they always had.

A note from the author

For as long as I can remember, I have loved reading mystery books. It started with Enid Blyton's Famous Five, and The Secret Seven. As I got older, I progressed to Agatha Christie books, and of course, Sir Arthur Conan Doyle's Sherlock Holmes.

I love the characters of Sherlock Holmes and Dr Watson, and the Victorian era that the stories are set in. It seemed only natural that one day, I would write some of my own Sherlock stories. I love creating new mysteries for Mr Holmes, and his trusty companion, Dr John Watson. It's not just the era itself that seems to ignite ideas within me; it's also the characters who were around at that time, and the lives they led.

This story has been checked for errors, but if you see anything we have missed and you'd like to let us know about them, please email mabel@mabelswift.com

You can hear about my new releases by signing up to my newsletter www.mabelswift.com   As a thank you for subscribing, I will send you a free short story: Sherlock Holmes and The Curious Clock.

If you'd like to contact me, you can get in touch via mabel@mabelswift.com I'd be delighted to hear from you.

Best wishes

Mabel

Printed in Great Britain
by Amazon